Are you all here?

Mary Waesche Alessi
Cathy Fosnot

Illustration by Manuela Pentangelo

We dedicate this book to our children and grandchildren, who continually stimulate and challenge us to keep our minds creative.

Rhoda Red had 5 healthy, wonderful, fun-loving chicks.

They weren't always perfect, but she loved them with all her heart. "Ruby, Riley, Rose, Rubin and Roy...," Rhoda called out joyfully to her 5 chicks as she poked her head into the barn. "Are you all here?"

"Come on everyone, we're going into the barnyard to play. But remember, ... "

Rhoda cautioned them, "stay close, and don't go off on your own. I saw that crafty, old fox this morning, and he looked hungry!"

The 5 chicks lined up behind their mother and scurried into the yard.

Once in the barnyard, the chicks raced about scratching in the dirt to find some worms.

They were so involved in their search, they soon found themselves at different ends of the barnyard trying to determine who had found the juiciest worm.

Rhoda Red was carefully keeping an eye out for the crafty, old fox.

She turned around to make sure her babies were safe.

"Oh, no, no, no, no, no! What happened?" Rhoda Red screamed. Had the hungry fox taken one of her babies?

She knew they were all there when they walked to the barnyard in a straight line, but now things looked very different.

Rhoda called out in a worried voice, "Ruby, Riley, Rose, Rubin and Roy.... are you all here?"

Are they?

With a quizzical look, Ruby, Riley, and Rose shouted, "We're right here, Mom. What's the matter?"

Rubin yelled, "I'm here, too!" Roy yelled, too, but no one heard him because he was a little busy.

"Oh, thank goodness, you are all here!"
Rhoda Red exclaimed.
"I thought for sure that fox
had come when I wasn't
looking and taken one of you."

Rhoda Red had been very worried, but now
she relaxed a little knowing all her 5
babies were there,
safe and sound.

here!

"Let's have a race to the stable," said Riley.

"OK," said Rose, "but I get a head start because I'm the smallest."

Ruby, Riley, Rubin and Roy got behind the starting line.

Rose moved a few chicken feet
ahead of the rest and when
everyone was in position,
she turned around and yelled,

"Mom, can you start the race?"

Rhoda turned around,
about to say "Go,"
but instead she said,
"Oh, no, no, no, no, no. Not again!"

They were all here before,
when she had seen 3 and 2
earlier, but now she saw
only 4 chicks on the
starting line,
with Rose out in front.

"Ruby, Riley, Rose, Rubin and Roy...are you all here?" Are they?

All the chicks yelled at once, "Come on Mom! Stop worrying. We're all here." And so they were.

"Oh, thank goodness, you are all here," exclaimed Rhoda with relief. "I know that fox is around here somewhere and I worry about you."

Rhoda Red took a deep breath and began to relax. She got into character as the referee and with her wing poised high in the air,

she lowered it quickly, yelling

"Go kids, go!"

Rose got an early lead, but Ruby, Riley and Rubin were close behind.

Roy... well, along the way he had gotten a little distracted and was at the back of the group.

Little Rose won the race by a mere beak length in front of her other siblings.

After the race, the chicks started laughing and talking about how their mother was acting so worried every time they formed different groups.

"Let's do it again," said Rose mischievously.

Ruby and Riley huddled together by the pig pen, while Rubin and Roy ducked behind the cow's legs.

In order to get their mom's attention, Rose threw a big rock into a puddle and made a big splash.

The sound of the splash made Rhoda Red jump!

She turned around so fast she got dizzy and fell down.

Looking up in horror, she saw her chicks grouped differently again.

"Oh, no, no, no, no, no!" She yelled.
  "Not again!"
She was certain the fox had come this time
and taken one of her babies. With fear in her
voice, she slowly called out, "Ruby, Riley, Rose,
Rubin and Roy ... are you all here?"

Are they?

Ruby, Riley, Rose, Rubin and Roy were all hysterical.

They were laughing so hard they could hardly breathe.

Finally, Rose calmed down enough to say, "We're all here Mom. Don't worry."

All 5 chicks were
safe and sound and
Rhoda was relieved.
But, she did not appreciate
their antics!
"It's not funny! I've had enough!"
she said with a frown.
"I thought for sure the fox had come and
taken one of you away."

"Everyone come here,"
Rhoda demanded.

With her 5 babies safely tucked under her wings, Rhoda Red thought about all the ways her chicks had grouped themselves together.

"I get it now," she thought. "There are many way they can group themselves. Just because they changed groups doesn't mean that I had lost any of them to that nasty fox. They were here the whole time."

"OK,"
said Rhoda Red,
"everybody, back to the barn."
Ruby, Riley, Rose, Rubin and Roy
all raced back to the barn shouting,
"Last one in eats a stinky bug."

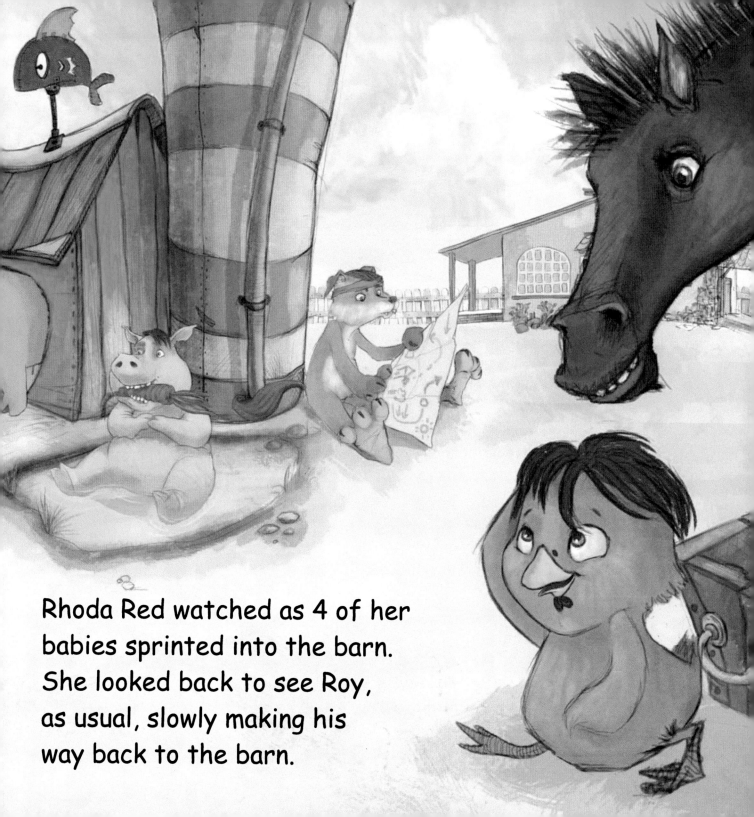

Rhoda Red watched as 4 of her babies sprinted into the barn. She looked back to see Roy, as usual, slowly making his way back to the barn.

"Well," said Rhoda,
"there are 4 in the barn
and 1 slow poke.

But this time ...
I know all my babies are safe
and sound, because 4 + 1 makes 5.
All my chicks are here.
I'm not going to worry about the fox this time."

Should she be worried?

"That's strange," said Rhoda. She had an odd feeling that something just wasn't right. Just to be sure, she decided to count her babies one more time. She had each chick call out a number.

"1," said Ruby.
"2," said Riley.
"3," said Rose.
"4," said Rubin.
"5," said Roy.

"OK, so now I know all my babies
are here, safe and sound,"
said Rhoda.

"But wait! What's this?
There's one more!
What??"
shouted Rhoda.

"I don't have 6 baby chicks!"

"Oh, no, no, no, no, no!
No, you don't!!"

Printed in the United States of America
First Printing, 2017

    ISBN-10: 0-9976886-5-3
    ISBN-13: 978-0-9976886-5-8

Catherine Fosnot and Associates
New Perspectives on Learning, LLC
www.newperspectivesonlearning.com

About the Authors

Mary Waesche Alessi

Mary Waesche Alessi is a Registered Nurse by profession, but she also holds a degree in Early Childhood Education. With 5 preschool and kindergarten aged grandchildren, who all listen to and love her storytelling, Mary quickly discovered that she had a talent for weaving math learning opportunities into her stories with creative, fun, imaginative story lines. *Are You All Here?* is her first published book for children. She is currently working on a sequel, *The Gang's All Here.*

Cathy Fosnot

Cathy Fosnot is Professor Emerita of Childhood Education from CCNY, where she was the founder of the acclaimed center, Mathematics in the City. She has authored numerous books and articles on mathematics education, most recently *Conferring with Young Mathematicians at Work: Making Moments Matter* and the *Contexts for Learning Mathematics* series, K-6, a curriculum used widely by schools around the world. In 2004 she received the Teacher of the Year award from CCNY. Currently she serves as the senior content consultant for the award-winning internet math environment, DreamBox Learning, and is the President of New Perspectives on Learning, New Perspectives Online, and New Perspectives on Assessment. She resides in New London, CT, where she frequently offers workshops with her team at Ocean Beach.

About the Illustrator

Manuela Pentangelo

Manuela Pentangelo is an illustrator who loves to paint and create. Her passion for illustration has led her to have more than 40 published children's books available in many countries around the world and in many formats (print, animations, online, tablet). Her style is a combination of traditional and digital painting. She lives and works on The Island of the Island, a small island off the coast of Sardinia.

Made in United States
Orlando, FL
08 November 2022

24354753R00022